Sugar & Spice

—— ❋ ——

NATASHA KING

DENOR
PRESS

ISBN - 10: 0-9526056-2-7   ISBN - 13: 978-0-9526056-2-1

British Library Cataloguing in Publication Data.
A catalogue record of this publication is available from the
British Library.

American Library of Congress Register of Copyrights.

Published by Denor Press Ltd.
PO Box 12913, London, N12 8ZR
Email: denor@dial.pipex.com

Book cover, design and layout by Jonathan Phillips
www.toccatadesign.com

Printed by Lightning Source, Milton Keynes, UK

CONTENTS

— ❈ —

SUGAR & SPICE

Natasha King

— ❋ —

Natasha King is the pseudonym for Esther Orden. Born in South Africa, her life is a kaleidoscope of fascinating experiences and she regales audiences with her intriguing short stories.

As an international traveler, her path has been intense and her professions diverse! She started her career as a concert pianist (recorded the Schumann Piano Concerto with the SABC Orchestra), went on to qualify as a School Teacher at the Teachers' Training College, obtained the LTCL Music Degree (Piano), became South Africa's most successful "woman" private property developer, started the first Oscar Award Ceremony for South African Actors, initiated a 'sick visiting' program for hospitals as well as other communal benefits in her area, has helped many refugees and gave a scholarship for African students to study medicine during the difficult apartheid days in South Africa.

Esther Orden has worked as a Music Therapist in Cape Town and has lectured about music in both South Africa and the United Kingdom. She now lives in London in the UK where she continues to perform music, write and share her fascinating stories.

DEDICATION

To my children Lucille, Morris and Geoffrey,
my grandchildren Serena, Felicia and Joe
and
in memory of my husband, Dr Joseph Orden

Acknowledgements

I would like to express my thanks and appreciation for the support and encouragement of Ed Katz (Creative Writing, Cape Town), the team at Denor Press, Nicholas Stapleton, Veronica Nixon, Lyn Fuss, Frida Michaelson, Margarete Weiss and Daphne Claff

The Governess

— ❈ —

As a South African country doctor's wife, with the surgery attached to the house, I became familiar with all the patients. They were mostly farmers from the surrounding areas and travelled on long dusty roads or over the mountains to reach us. I was expected to welcome them, serve a tray of tea and have a little chat with each one. They were usually quite interesting people and I enjoyed the company.

One particular family interested me. Mrs Robertson was a fine looking woman, well educated and beautifully spoken. She suffered from a chronic back ailment. Her husband, a typical farmer, was the Chairman of the Farmers Association and was continually called upon to attend meetings all over the countryside. She often complained in conversation about being left alone on the farm with her three young children whilst her husband was on his travels.

Mrs Robertson decided to solve her problem of loneliness by engaging a governess to educate her boys on their farm, rather than sending them away to boarding school.

Unfortunately, retaining the long-term services of a governess proved impossible. The isolation of the farm was such that no-one would stay for more than a few weeks!

Poor Mrs Robertson would confide in me:
"Another new governess has arrived! I pray that this one

will remain for at least a year!"
Eventually, Providence provided! Marion, the new
governess, confessed that she loved the isolated and
peaceful farm life – so much so that even on her free days,
she never once visited town or sought to accompany
Mr Robertson on the occasional outing to the nearest
village.

Mrs Robertson sang her praises.
"Marion is an excellent teacher and so helpful to me as well.
She is a marvellous masseuse, regularly treating my painful
back and insisting on my safety, helps me in and out of the
bath. She is a real gem."

I was delighted to hear the news and happy that this
governess had stayed well over the year.

One day Mrs Robertson telephoned me, sounding quite
hysterical.
"You'll never believe it!" she sobbed, "Marion has gone!
Yesterday four men unexpectedly arrived at the farm and
asked for Marion. I called her and to my astonishment they
rushed up to her and, after a scuffle, they handcuffed her!"

Mrs Robinson continued:
"I was standing there, rooted to the spot with shock, when
one of the men approached me."
"'Do not be afraid, Mrs Robertson. I am from the South
African Police and am accompanying these three American
detectives who have traced Marion to your farm after
searching for her for two years. You see, she is actually a
man in disguise - and is wanted for first degree murder in
the United States!'"

The Choice

— ✸ —

When I lived in Durban, I had a charming neighbour, Alexa Orloff, a White Russian refugee. She was of the Russian aristocracy and had managed to escape when the Soviets took control of the country. She was a fine looking woman who wore magnificent jewellery, which she had managed to smuggle out of the country by sewing it into the hems of her coats.

Alexa fled to Shanghai, where she met the manager of an international photographic equipment company who controlled the business for the whole of the Far East. He fell in love with her and they married. Later, they came to live in Durban.

When I visited her, I noticed a very elaborate cradle in the bedroom. She explained to me that as she had no children, the cradle was used for her dog!

When war broke out, I moved from my home, as my husband had joined the army. I lost touch with her.

One day, a couple of years later, walking along the beachfront, I met her walking her dog. We decided to go and have a cup of tea together. When we were seated, I enquired:
"Well, what's new? How's your husband?"
"Oh, he was appointed Price Controller for Rhodesia (as it was

then) so he's living in Bulawayo." Her eyes filled with tears.
"And so?" I urged her to continue.

"Well, when he got the appointment, we were informed that we could not take Sergei (the dog) with us until he had been in quarantine for a year. I was horrified at the thought of parting from him for so long and could not possibly agree to anything like that!
Therefore, we decided that my husband should go on his own. Whilst there, he fell in love with his secretary and only returned to Durban to arrange a divorce from me, in order to marry her!"

Alexa sat and wept whilst I remained silent, wondering how any woman could give up a fine husband for a dog, no matter how much she loved it!

However, I was soon to be enlightened.
"You must understand, Natasha," she said between sobs, "I realised that even though I loved him and would miss him, my husband was able to survive independently – but it would be quite impossible for poor Sergei to look after himself!"

Double Check!

— ✳ —

Reading Shalom Aleichem's "The Town of the Little People," brought to mind an incident my dear late mother always quoted. It occurred in a similar 'shtetel' (little village) in Poland, where she grew up.

As a child, she lived in a small village, inhabited mainly by people of poor means, as was typical of those days at the end of the nineteenth century. There were no shops of significance but that problem was solved by a large trap and horses which would leave from the village square every second Monday to travel to the nearest large town, about ten miles away, returning in the late afternoon. This service was indeed a vital necessity for my mother's large family.

One Monday morning, her mother (my grandmother) sent her to the large town to do some really urgent shopping for the family. She left the house, as she thought, well on time. However, as she walked hurriedly down the street, she bumped into her friend, Jan.
"Where you rushing to?" Jan enquired.
"To catch the shopping trap and horses," my mother answered as she rushed by.
"You've just missed it!" Jan shouted after her. "I saw it leave ten minutes ago!"
Mother was shattered and turned back home.

"What are you doing back here?" upbraided my grandmother.

"Oh, I am so sorry, but I met Jan and he told me that the trap had already left," Mother responded tearfully, as she knew how critical the shopping errand was.
"Run quickly and check for yourself if that is really so – there is still time before the scheduled departure. You never know, Jan could have made a mistake!" shrieked my grandmother.

Mother dashed off to the village square. To her great relief, the trap was still there, preparations still being made for its departure! When she returned home that evening, her mother counselled:
"You see, my daughter, never accept negative information from others when you are capable of checking the truth for yourself. Let that be a lesson for life!"

This story and the lesson learned has been handed down to four subsequent generations in my family! We apply the lesson "across the board" and have been saved many a disappointment!

The Law is an Ass

— ❈ —

Some years ago I was a permanent resident at a five-star hotel in Durban. I noticed, at a table close to me in the dining room, a smart, good looking lady of about forty years of age.

She entertained the finest people of the town, and I was particularly interested to note that bank managers were her most frequent company for dinner.

Over time, we developed quite a friendship. She spoke with a fascinating French accent and informed me that she was the daughter of the Contesse de Laroche of Paris, indicating that she came from the finest aristocracy of France.

One day she approached me, saying:
"I have been invited to an important party at the French Embassy tonight and as I did not bring any furs in my baggage from Paris, I was wondering whether you would mind lending me that lovely mink stole I have seen you wearing, as it is so chilly today."
 How could I refuse?
"Of course," I reassured her, "Come upstairs and get it right away."

But somehow that night I felt unhappy about it.
"What if she loses it? What if she does not return it?"
 I would have no redress and I certainly would be very sad

never to wear it again. I really could not sleep for worrying about it!

But, lo and behold, at the crack of dawn there was a knock on my door, and there she was, with the fur, thanking me profusely.

I felt rather ashamed of my ugly thoughts!

A few days later, on a Saturday morning, she ran up to me as I was getting into my car, waving a cheque and calling: "As you are going into town, would you be kind enough to change this cheque for me at the Bank, as I must have this money urgently today and I cannot get away to attend to it?" The cheque was for five hundred pounds.

I took the cheque to my Bank, but the teller said: "I'm sorry but as this is a country bank cheque, I cannot pay it out as that bank is closed today and I cannot confirm it. However, if this is a friend of yours and you wish to guarantee it for her, I will pay it out."

Having in mind my mean thoughts about the fur I had loaned her, I immediately agreed to his suggestion and took the cash back to the hotel. She was extremely grateful.

The following morning at daybreak there was a loud knocking noise at my door. There she was, fully dressed, with eyes full of tears, sobbing her heart out.

"Oh my dear," she cried, "I've just had a terrible 'phone call – my dear husband has been involved in a shocking accident and is not expected to live. I have to rush back to the country, hoping to get there before he dies. Goodbye, goodbye – I'll let you know what happens!"

The following day was Monday. At nine-thirty in the

morning I received a telephone call from the Bank. "Come immediately! The Manager wants to see you!" As I entered his office he rose to greet me, saying: "There's a mug born every minute!"

"What's this all about?" I asked.
"Well, my dear, you are the latest victim of that French Countess – every Bank Manager in this town has been 'caught' by her, so you're in very good company. That cheque she gave you – well, she has never had an account at that Bank. They don't even know her name and – by the way – she has never had a husband either!"

The Bank Manager insisted on laying a charge of theft against her.

To my surprise she returned to Durban about three months later and the police picked her up and charged her. I was called to attend court.

The Magistrate first heard my story and then she went into the box. To my amazement, she appeared dressed as if she was off to a garden party – the essence of smartness and good taste.
"It's all a misunderstanding," she pleaded. "Would I, the daughter of the great French Countess de Laroche, stoop to run off with five hundred miserable pounds? No French aristocrat would do such a thing – never!" (The tears were wiped away with a beautiful lace handkerchief.)
"The money will be paid back immediately – the moment we both leave the court."

The Magistrate was so impressed with her beauty, her

smartness, her lovely French accent and aristocratic bearing that he unmercifully upbraided me.
"How dare you think badly of this fine aristocratic lady? It's a complete misunderstanding. Case dismissed!"

Needless to say, many years later, I am still waiting for my money.

The Law is an Ass!

Music is the Food of Love... and Hate

— ✳ —

The concert had been advertised in the Durban newspaper.

"The eminent concert pianist Katherine Goddard will perform the Schumann Piano Concerto in A minor with the Durban Symphony Orchestra under the baton of the internationally acclaimed Viennese conductor Alfred Zimmerman: Durban City Hall, 8pm, Sunday 15 May."

My party and I arrived in good time and we sat in the centre of the second row, impatiently waiting for the piano concerto to be performed after the interval.

The guest conductor from Vienna, Alfred Zimmerman, was young and handsome, dynamic and capable. The orchestra was in fine fettle, the hall was packed to full capacity and there was a buzz of appreciation and excited anticipation.

At last it was time for the piano concerto to be performed. The large concert grand was moved to the front of the stage. Katherine, glamorous in a stunning scarlet designer gown, made her entrance, bowed to the audience and took her place at the piano.

The conductor nodded to her, bowed slightly to the orchestra, took up his baton and commenced the orchestral introduction to the concerto. As it came to an end, he turned to Katherine, leading her in with the haunting melodic announcement of the piano part. She played divinely, producing exquisite tones which touched my very soul.

Suddenly a middle-aged woman, sitting in the front row just ahead of us, began coughing loudly and relentlessly, creating a cruel and unnerving disturbance.

The audience began to hiss in distress. The conductor, still holding his beat, turned to face the audience. But the incessant, ghastly coughing persisted.

Suddenly, Katherine stopped playing and turned towards the guilty woman with at first a horrified and then an appealing expression on her face. Intriguingly, the woman immediately stopped coughing.

Katherine then nodded to the conductor and they recommenced the concerto.

After about ten minutes of heavenly music-making, the coughing started all over again. On this occasion, Katherine arose from the piano stool and with tears streaming down her face, ran off the stage and disappeared into the wings.

The conductor turned to the audience and apologised, explaining that it was quite impossible to perform with the continuous interruption of the loud coughing. The woman responsible then simply stood up and walked out of the hall.

The next day, on making enquiries, Alfred Zimmerman was given Katherine's address. He wanted to call on her and discuss the unbelievable events of the previous evening. He rang the doorbell of her home and she herself answered the door. When she saw who was there, she burst into tears. He put his arms around her, saying:
"Please let me come in and speak to you. I am so upset at what happened last night. I could murder that woman for upsetting you and ruining our concert. Who is she? What does she want?"

"Oh", sobbed Katherine, "you will find it difficult to believe but she is my mother and this is her way of punishing me! You see, when she and my father were divorced, I chose to live with him as he encouraged my interest in music whereas she was completely indifferent to it. I can do nothing about it - she has started to stalk and follow me everywhere I perform, to take her revenge."

Zimmerman was duly shocked at her own mother's merciless behaviour. Sympathising with Katherine, he ended up taking her out for dinner that night. They developed an ever growing closeness and love for each other during his three-month contract in South Africa and when he was due to leave, he asked her to marry him!

Katherine now lives happily in Vienna, far away from her brutal mother, performing regularly under the baton of her handsome and adoring husband. To "adapt" Shakespeare's immortal words:
".... music is the food of love...."

The Signal

I was the driver. My friend sat in the passenger seat of my enviable Lagonda coupe.

We reached a fork in the road and there at the junction was a policeman, standing on his box and officiously directing the traffic. I signalled to him, gesticulating my wish to take the left-hand fork. He signalled me to proceed to the left but as I passed him, he banged on the car, shouting at me to stop.

He was furious, asking me why I had not obeyed his signal! My passenger and I were adamant that he had waved me on to the left-hand fork and that I had obeyed that signal. He would not permit us to give any explanation, demanded our names and addresses and rudely shouted at me that I would be prosecuted for disobeying his command.

A few days later I duly received a Summons to attend Court. During the session, the policeman first presented his case, following which I was called upon to defend my actions. I did so, emphasising that the traffic policeman had signalled his agreement to my taking the left fork in the road, that I had obeyed his signal and even had a witness to prove it.

The Magistrate appeared incredulous and belligerently demanded:
"Are you trying to tell me that a traffic policeman would

give a wrong signal?"

"Yes, your Honour," I replied. "I read in the newspapers about murders and although I have never witnessed one, I know that they take place."

With that, the Magistrate drew himself up and pronounced in disgust:
"Case dismissed!"

A few days later I was invited to dinner at the fashionable Royal Hotel. In the restaurant, I noticed a great friend of mine, Louise, dining at a table with a number of traffic policemen! She called out:
"Hello, Natasha! Enjoy your dinner!" and then turned back to her company.

As I entered my home later that evening, the telephone was ringing – it was Louise. She warned me that the police had been discussing my very case over dinner. She told me that it was their avowed intention to "entrap" me and bring some criminal charge against me - by hook or by crook - in order to exonerate their colleague whom I had embarrassed in Court!

To this day I have evaded capture......... and after this passage of time, it is just a case of "catch me if you can!"

The
Front Door Key

— ❋ —

Natasha, a young librarian, lived in a beautiful block
of flats overlooking the sea, in Brighton. She was blonde
and gorgeous looking, had a very neat figure and a warm
and friendly manner. One day, in the library, she attended
to a client, who gave his address as the same building in
which she lived. His name was Desmond Phillips and to her
surprise, after their initial meeting, he frequently 'popped'
into the library to chat with her.

She thought he was terrific and very charming and she
anxiously anticipated that he would extend an invitation
to her to go out together. She found herself falling in love
with him and was bitterly disappointed that he never ever
suggested a date.

One day, in the library, he said, "I'm leaving early
tomorrow morning on holiday to visit my brother in France
and expect to spend the next six months with him as we
have a great deal of family business to attend to. I would
like to leave my key with you and ask you to go into my flat
(no 49) and water my few plants, perhaps once or twice a
week." Natasha happily agreed and he walked out without
any further discussion.

She rushed home at five o'clock expecting him to call at

any moment and give her his key. Late at night, she thought she heard some rustling at her door but when she opened it, there was no one there.

She went to bed very heartsore and disappointed and the following morning went off to work at the usual time, wondering why he had obviously changed his mind. She frequently thought of him during the next six months, but was just completely puzzled at his behaviour.

Desmond eventually returned home after six months and was disappointed and disgusted when he found his beautiful plants had died!
As a result, when he saw her at the library or in the building, he snubbed her and looked the other way.
Poor Natasha could not understand the whole issue but she had no means of finding out the truth of the matter.

At the end of the year Natasha decided to move to London, where some of her family lived. She was very lonely. She decided to sell her flat. The buyer did not want to take over any carpets or curtains. When the movers came, Natasha told them to take up all the fitted carpets including the small specialised dust catcher in the entrance hall, just inside the front door.

As they removed that little piece of carpet, she spotted a crumpled, white envelope with her name on it, lying under it. She picked it up and opened it.
"Dear Natasha," she read, "I am enclosing my key as discussed with you and I will greatly appreciate your attention to my plants. I have been rather shy in my approach to you but that is my nature! However, I promise

you that we will get together as soon as I return home and you can expect a great time with me! With fondest love, Desmond."

Natasha was horrified! She made up her mind to go and see him that very night and explain the terrible mishap.
This she did...............and "they lived happily ever after!"

When Your Ship Comes In

— ❋ —

Many years ago I was teaching at a school in Doornfontein, Johannesburg. Russian immigrants settled near the school, and I was called upon not only to teach them but also to assist them in adjusting to their new lives.

I was very surprised to find a Russian medical doctor amongst the newcomers. I taught his young daughter, Edna, and became good friends with his family.

After a while, Dr Schand was advised to go over to London to take the necessary medical exams in order to practice in South Africa.

His family managed to scrape together sufficient money to buy a one-way ticket to travel 'steerage' on a ship to London. He had a bunk in the bowels of the ship in a cabin housing ten other men! They were, of course, a dirty and noisy crowd and he was most out of place amongst them.

After a few days at sea, the ship's purser sent for him. He went up to the purser's office in fear and trembling, wondering what he was wanted for and praying that there was no trouble in the offing.

"Good morning, Doctor," said the purser, very sternly. "Tell me, have you practised medicine for many years?"
"Oh yes," Dr Schand replied. "I was working in a big hospital in Moscow for ten years and came in contact with the finest professors and surgeons in the Soviet Union."
"Well," came the reply, "it sounds as if you are just the person we need!"

Dr Schand looked at him in astonishment, wondering what it was all about.

"You see," said the purser, "we have Sir John Eccles and his entourage travelling with us. Unfortunately, his Lordship suffered a very bad attack of illness last night and our ship's doctor says that if he is not operated upon immediately, he has no hope of survival. Now, I want to ask you to assist at the operation as this is our only hope to save his life."

The operation was immediately arranged and Dr Schand assisted the ship's doctor in the challenging surgery.

Fortunately, the operation was successful and the patient was eventually returned to his suite.

Dr Schand was allowed to visit him daily and soon a pleasant friendship developed between Sir John and Dr Schand.

A few days before the ship was due to dock at Southampton, Sir John said to Dr Schand:
"I do want to thank you for all your help and interest in my health and would like to show my appreciation. Do tell me what your plans are in London."

Dr Schand explained his purpose in going over to London and Sir John was interested to hear about it.

"How will you manage financially?" he asked.

"Oh, it's a great struggle, but I'll come through alright. I'll work at night as a waiter or something and attend medical school during the day. I'll get through, as many poor students do!"

Sir John was fascinated.

"Now listen," he said. "I will help you, just as you kindly helped me. Come and be my guest for a couple of weeks and then I will arrange accommodation for you. I will also consider it a privilege to pay for all your studies."

He kept his word and saw Dr Schand through that difficult year. When the time came for him to return to South Africa, Sir John surprised him and paid for his return voyage. By coincidence, it was the very same ship on which he had come to England – but this time, instead of being in cramped 'steerage', he travelled in the luxury and comfort of First Class!

Eye of the Storm

— ❋ —

The silence of the night was shattered by the shrill ringing of the telephone. My country doctor husband and I were awakened with a start. The rain was beating against the windows, the wind was howling and lightning and thunder created a truly wild atmosphere.

My husband took the call and then said to me:
"It was Mr Jones from the Inn at Botha's Hill. The telephone reception was crackling and unclear because of the storm but I think that he said that a person has had an accident and his eye has been knocked out. I could not hear anything else so I had better go and investigate."

I was very worried at the idea of him travelling at night on the long, dirt road to Botha's Hill, especially given the awful weather, but I accepted that it was 'all in the day's work.'
He returned a few hours later and told me what had occurred.

When he arrived at the Inn, it was all in darkness and he had to bang and kick on the front door for some time before Mr Jones, holding a lamp in his hand, peered out and opened the door.
"What are you doing here, Doc?" he shouted over the whistling wind.
"Well, I came to see the person who has damaged his eye,"

replied my husband.

"Oh no, I did not say a *person*, I said a *Persian* – a cat!" he laughed. "So you had better go straight home again."

My husband was a lover of animals, so he suggested:

"Well, let me have a look at the cat and see if I can help him in any way."

On examination, as the eye was severely damaged, my husband gave the cat an anaesthetic and removed the damaged eye. He left the 'patient' sleeping quite comfortably.

A week later, he returned to see how the cat was doing and was shocked when the owner said to him:

"Look Doc, I can't bear the sight of that cat without his eye. Do me a favour, 'put him down' and I'll be rid of him. I'm begging you to relieve me of the sight of him!"

My husband was shocked.

"Oh no," he said, "I wouldn't dream of doing such a thing! I help people to live, not to die! But if you like, I'll take him home with me and care for him."

"Please do," retorted Mr Jones, "and I'll be glad to be shot of him for ever."

And so my husband brought the beautiful Persian cat home and we nursed him back to good health. He led a happy and long life, and was utterly devoted to my husband; waiting at the front door each day to welcome him on his arrival home and then following him everywhere.

You could say that the cat 'kept an eye out' for him!

The Silver Hand-Mirror

— ✳ —

As a young child, I loved to play with the hand-mirror on my mother's dressing-table.
It was made of solid silver and was very beautiful.

One day I noticed, to my dismay, that it was missing. My mother explained that she had given it to a dear friend who had recently come to visit her in South Africa, from far-away Czechoslovakia.

I missed the mirror terribly and occasionally mentioned this to my mother. She, however, always remarked that she was happy to have given it to Marina, who was now experiencing a difficult time, as her country was at war with Russia.

Many years passed and eventually my mother left South Africa to travel in Europe. Whilst there, she decided to go to Czechoslovakia and visit Marina.

Mother was greeted with great enthusiasm by her friend, who kept repeating during her stay:
"You have saved my life! Thank you! Thank you!" The tears ran down her face as she spoke these words.

Eventually my mother realized that there was more to this statement than just the pleasure of her visit.

" What do you mean?" asked my mother curiously.

"Well," said Marina, "during the war, a rough-looking Russian soldier turned up here one day, and barked: "I have been ordered to collect all your jewellery and valuables and bring them to the army barracks. If you do not willingly hand these over, my orders are to shoot you and all your family and bring your bodies to the captain!"

Marina continued: "I screamed at him that we had nothing left to give him as his men had already been here and confiscated all our valuable possessions!"

"I don't believe you," he snarled. "I'll have a good look around. Give me your keys!"

The story unfolded. He went into the bedrooms and opened the cupboards, but found nothing. As he was leaving the room, revolver in hand, his eye caught the hand-mirror on the dressing table. He picked it up and turned it over, admiring the silver.

"This is quite fine," he muttered. "I think that the captain would like to use this when trimming his beard and moustache."

So, grinning, he replaced his gun in its holster, concealed the mirror under his jacket - and walked out!

Variations on a Theme

— ✻ —

My daughter, Lucy, returned from Vienna where she had been studying piano at the Conservatoire under the finest European professors. She was engaged by a Durban orchestra to play a concerto, but being full of enthusiasm, she offered to play two concertos at the same concert! This was unheard of for any performer, since to be the soloist in only one concerto requires tremendous effort. I was therefore shocked when I heard of her decision but kept quiet as I did not want to dampen her enthusiasm.

The day of the concert arrived. Lucy was busy all day at the piano. Late in the afternoon, I went into the music room to call her to come and start dressing and to eat a light snack.
To my amazement, when I came up to the piano, I saw tears running down her face.
"What's wrong?" I asked.
"I can't play a single bar!" she burst out. "How could you do this to me?" she shrieked.

"What did I do?" I asked.
"Well, as you were a performer yourself, you know what hell it is to be a concert soloist and yet you have always encouraged me to follow this exacting profession! I'll never forgive you!"

I kept silent. She dressed and we left for the concert hall. Needless to say, she played divinely and the newspapers praised her highly as a very talented young pianist who would go far. Indeed, she spent the next few years travelling internationally and performing successfully.

Several years later, she had married and was expecting the arrival of a baby. The child was born during the night and I arrived at the hospital in the early morning and went straight to my daughter's room.

"What's your baby like?" I asked.
"Oh Mummy," my daughter cried ecstatically, "she's got the most wonderful musician's hands!"

It was all I could do not to burst out laughing as my mind went back ten years to the evening that she had performed the two concertos and had admonished me so! I didn't say a word or remind her how cruel she had thought me for encouraging music as a profession!

Addendum
It is clear that true musical talent will out!
This baby grand-daughter eventually became a concert violinist but in the reverse of my experience, she berates her mother for not encouraging her performing career more whilst she was a child.

As a psychologist once quipped,
"There are only two types of parents, and they are both wrong!"

Masquerade

— ✳ —

I turn over the pages of a family album and stop at a photograph taken on board ship, a luxury Italian liner, which travelled regularly up the east coast of Africa from Cape Town to Venice.

I boarded the vessel in Durban with my young daughter. To our absolute amazement, the moment that we stepped on deck a beautiful, smart, middle-aged lady rushed up to me, pulling away from a small group of people. She embraced me and kissed me and my child, all the while exclaiming in a loud voice:
"How lovely to see you both again, my dears. I'm so glad we are travelling together. We will have such a grand time all the way to Venice."

Needless to say, I looked at her in amazement, thinking it was a case of mistaken identity. She then burst out:
"Oh, I never can remember your married name, so please help me, dear cousin."
Bemused, I 'reminded' her of my name and she introduced me all round saying:
"I told you my cousin would be joining this ship and I would be spending all my time with her, so here she is at last. Come, let's walk round the deck," she added, as she put her arm through mine and led me away from the crowd.

As soon as we were on our own, she drew close and

whispered:

"Please forgive me for what I did, but you surely will, once I have explained the circumstances. Every time I travel I have the same situation, so I have to protect myself. Because of my unusual title, I am the Countess Giovanna Strauss, I find that all sorts of people try to attach themselves to me for the whole of the journey. So I start off by saying I am awaiting a relative to join me on board, with whom I am 'obliged' to spend all my time during the trip. So when I saw you, I felt you were just the person to fill that niche – hence my effusive greeting to you and now, if you don't mind, you will have to put up with my devoted company for the rest of the voyage!"

As it turned out, she was fascinating and delightful company, and because of my 'relationship' with her, I was thoroughly spoiled by the staff and had the best cruise of my life.

Smiling, I close the album on the beautiful portrait of 'Vanna', the exotic Austrian countess, which had so vividly re-kindled memories of my unique and unforgettable 'cousin'!

Christmas Story

— ✳ —

My neighbour was a friendly soul. Ben Cohen was a middle-aged man, a widower, with a young son of about ten years of age.

One day, he confided that he was soon to be married to a very charming young widow, who was the mother of a nice young boy, about the same age as his own son. He was very happy about the marriage, the only obstacle being that she was not Jewish. They had talked about it and decided not to interfere with each other's faith, each continuing to attend the synagogue and church, as always.

One morning Ben called in to see me, very worried. It was a few days before Christmas and Jane, his fiancée, was arranging to have her usual Christmas tree in the centre of her lounge. Ben was worried. It was so different to his belief but he felt that it would not be fair to deny her this custom.

"What should I do, Natasha?" he fretted.
We discussed the situation, but could not come to any satisfactory conclusion. He then returned home, rather distraught ... only to find that Jane had given him a surprise and put the Christmas tree in the middle of his lounge!

That night, there was a loud knocking on my front door.

There was Ben, grinning from ear to ear.
"I've solved it!" he shouted, "and Jane is quite delighted!
I've placed a large 'Magen David' (a Star of David) on top
of the tree!"

A Wise Man Knows his Father

— ❋ —

Whilst I was a student at The Teacher's Training College in Johannesburg, a young lady approached me.

"I believe that your name is Natasha King - am I correct?" she asked.

"Yes," I said, "and who are you?"

"I am Sonia Shulley. I wanted to ask you if you have a sister who teaches at the Government School."

"Yes I do," I said.

"Well, I have a young brother, Abe, in her class and he is always talking about her."

That night I mentioned the incident to my sister. She raised her hands in horror and said "Don't mention Abe Shulley to me! He's the plague of my life, disobedient, stupid and cheeky - an absolute horror in the classroom!"

Needless to say, I avoided his sister at college and was surprised when she rushed over to me one day and said:

"I really must talk to you as I have something quite priceless to tell you. The only thing is, you must promise me that you will not repeat it to your sister."

Naturally intrigued, I promised.

She then continued:

"It appears that Abe had been behaving very badly in the

classroom. In desperation your sister sent him to the
headmaster for a good caning. She sent the class prefect
with him to accompany him as far as the Principal's office."

Abe knocked on the Principal's door, and entered the office
alone.
"Yes Shulley," said Mr Abrahams. "What do you want?
Have you come for a good caning for bad behaviour?"
"Oh no Sir," said Abe in a gentle voice. "Please Sir, Miss
King's watch has stopped and she wants to know the
correct time."

Mr Abrahams looked aghast.
"Tell Miss King it's eleven o'clock and that she had better
buy a new watch promptly. Now get out!"

Abe walked out of the door rubbing his behind and wiping
his downcast eyes. The prefect walked him back to the
classroom where he continued his act of remorse.

My sister never suspected a thing.

Now, fifty years later, I was dining at my daughter's London
home. Her husband, a busy doctor at a London Hospital,
arrived home with a middle-aged colleague. My
son-in-law introduced him to us, explaining that he was
newly appointed to the staff and had just arrived from
South Africa.

During dinner I asked the visitor:
"What part of SA do you come from?"
"Johannesburg is my home," he said.
"I did not catch your name. What is it?" I enquired.

"Shulley," he replied.

My grandson, who had been told the story of the naughty
schoolboy many a time, burst out laughing at the name.
"Do you know an Abe Shulley by any chance?" he asked.

"That's my father," he replied, quizzical at the general
merriment this evoked.
I need hardly tell you that once I had got my breath back
from laughing, I could not resist regaling him with the story
of that naughty schoolboy.
"Just like my father!" he said as he joined us in the laughter!

A Close Encounter

— ✻ —

I was spending a holiday on a farm in the Bethal area.
The house was typical of those days, fairly comfortable
but lacking in modern amenities. There was no electricity.
Paraffin lamps and candles were the order of the day. There
was no running water (water was collected in rain tanks)
and of course no indoor sanitation.

The "toilet hut" was situated some distance from the
house, down an overgrown path. It was a rough tin
contraption with a wooden door which left about twelve
to fifteen inches open at the top and the bottom, for air and
ventilation. There was a simple bolt to ensure privacy.

It was a stiflingly hot day, which was quite typical of the
South African summer weather. On one occasion, I visited
the toilet, locking the door after entering. All was peaceful
and quiet, as was to be expected.

Suddenly, I heard a peculiar rustling sound outside the door.
I looked down........and was horrified to see the huge head of
a hideous, large, black snake slithering through the aperture,
its tongue flickering! Slowly the entire snake wound itself
into sinuous loops on the floor of the toilet.
My immediate reflex was to lift my feet into the air above
it..... and scream! I screamed and screamed and then I
realised that no one could help me, even if they did hear me!

What was I to do? Initially I felt completely impotent but fortunately the survival instinct prevailed and I soon realised that I must pull myself together if I was to come out alive.

I jumped up onto the seat, leaned over to release the door bolt, sprung clear over the enormous reptile and dashed towards the house, yelling, "Snake! Snake!!"

Hearing my screams, the gardeners came running with spades and forks to combat the snake. It rose up menacingly onto its tail, poised to attack! However, the men managed to strike it down and eventually overpowered it.

They told me that it was very rare for anyone to escape with their life after such a close encounter - and that I should offer up a prayer of thanks for my miraculous escape!

A striking Mamba never misses!

Double Entendre

— ❋ —

When I first arrived in Cape Town, I gave a music lecture to a cultural association. Afterwards, I was offered a lift home by one of the members. Jack was a fine looking, elderly gentleman and we ended up with him arranging to take me to his rummy school, which met every Wednesday night. And so we gradually became good friends.

I had recently acquired a new apartment and Jack had been helping me look for the new furniture I would need. I was also looking for a good piano.

One morning, he telephoned:
"I'll be up to see you at eight o'clock tonight, Natasha."
And with that, he abruptly put down the phone.

I was completely bamboozled, but at eight o'clock he arrived with a gorgeous bunch of red roses. We went straight into the living room and sat down together on the settee.

 "Thank for letting me come," he said. "It's about the piano that you'll be needing."
After taking a deep breath, Jack took my hand and whilst clasping it tightly to his breast, continued:
"When my wife died, about ten years ago, I sold my big home with all my furniture, except for two articles - my grand piano and my double bed, which I have kept in

storage all this time. Now Natasha, I want to offer you both these articles, but the offer is...that you should share them with me.
I hope you will agree to do so, as I have fallen deeply in love with you."

I was rather shocked, but pulling myself together, responded:
"Thank you for the kind offer. You have sprung quite a surprise on me, Jack! However, I will gladly accept the offer of a grand piano – but you must give me a little more time to decide about the double bed!"

"Of course," he said.
With that, he left without another word.

I took the grand piano but will leave the rest to your imagination!

Printed in the United Kingdom
by Lightning Source UK Ltd.
116874UKS00001B/226-240